British Library Cataloguing in Publication Data

McCullagh, Sheila K.
    Christmas in Puddle Lane. — (Puddle Lane).
    I. Title   II. Dillow, John   III. Series
    428.6   PE1119
    ISBN 0-7214-9581-8

First edition

Published by Ladybird Books Ltd Loughborough Leicestershire UK
Ladybird Books Inc Lewiston Maine 04240 USA

Printed in England

Christmas
in Puddle Lane

written by SHEILA McCULLAGH
illustrated by JOHN DILLOW

Ladybird Books

One cold winter's evening, the Magician
was sitting by his fire, when the window
blew open, and the barn owl flew in.
"I have news, Magician," cried the owl.
"News from the magical Country of Zorn.
Old Margarita is ill. She needs your help."

The Magician could not only work magic,
he was also a very good doctor.
"I will go at once, Owl," he said.
He put on a thick cloak, and picked up
a red bag, covered in golden stars.
He went downstairs, and out into the cold wind.
So the Magician was away from home,
when the ice and snow came.

The wind dropped and it was very cold
in the Magician's garden.
When the cats, who lived under the steps
of the Magician's house, went fishing,
they found the stream covered in ice.

Then the snow came.
The sky grew black and the wind blew cold.
The snow fell all day and all night.
Sarah and Davy had to wear boots
to go out into Puddle Lane.

The mice who lived under
the hollow tree
began to get very hungry.
When the snow first fell,
they found a big cheese.
But when that was gone,
there was nothing else to eat.
The birds had eaten all the seeds,
and the snow went on falling,
until it was so deep
the mice had to tunnel
through it to get out.

As the days went on, they grew hungrier
and hungrier. They were so hungry that
they struggled over the snow
to the market building, looking for scraps.
But the snow was so deep, that no one
could get to market, and the little mice
went home hungrier than ever.

The children who lived in Puddle Lane
loved the snow. Whenever the sun was out,
they played outside in the snow.

One day, when the clouds were black
and the snow was falling,
Sarah and Davy made Christmas decorations.
"Let's make little red Christmas stockings
for everyone in Puddle Lane," said Sarah.
And she began to cut the stockings
out of a big piece of red cloth.

There was a knock at the door,
and Hari and Gita came in.
"What are you doing?" asked Hari.
"Making stockings for everyone in Puddle Lane,"
said Davy.
Hari and Gita sat down to help.
"I know what we could do," said Gita.
"Let's make a stocking for the mice
who live under the hollow tree.
They must be very hungry, in all this snow."
"I'll make one for the cats, too," said Sarah.
"I'm going to make a green stocking
for the Griffle," said Davy.
(The Griffle was a magical creature
who lived in the Magician's garden.)
"What are we going to put in them?"
asked Hari. "It's not much good having stockings
if there's nothing inside them."
"Let's make some little animals," said Sarah.
"We've got fir-cones and twigs and feathers."

So they all sat around the table,
making little animals to go in the stockings,
until it was time for Hari and Gita
to go home.

The next day, Hari and Gita arrived
with two little cakes.
"One is for the mice," said Gita.
"And one is for the Griffle."
They filled the stockings.
They put nuts and raisins in them all,
and cheese, wrapped in silver paper,
in the stocking for the mice.
Sarah put some brown bread, spread with
fishpaste, in the stocking for the cats.

They all went out into Puddle Lane,
and hung a red stocking
on the door of every house,
except their own.

They went into the Magician's garden,
and left a stocking for the cats
by the hole under the front steps.

Davy hung the stocking for the Griffle
on a tree.

They cleared the snow from the hollow tree,
and put the cake and the stocking
for the mice inside.

While the children were in the garden,
the Magician was coming back to Candletown.
Old Margarita was well again,
and he was coming home for Christmas.
He stopped at the ruined castle, and gave
the Gruffle, who lived there, a sack of coal.
(The Gruffle breathed fire and smoke,
so he ate coal, to stoke up his fire.)

As the Magician went under the archway
into Puddle Lane, he saw two green ears.
"Hello, Griffle," he said.
A green head came into view,
and there was the Griffle.

"I'm – I'm glad you're back," said the Griffle,
in his whiffly-griffly voice.
"So am I," said the Magician.
"What has been happening in Puddle Lane?"
"It's been very cold," said the Griffle.
"Mr Gotobed has been feeding the birds every day,
but the cats and the mice have been hungry."
"I'll get some food for them at once,"
said the Magician.
"It's all right now," said the Griffle.
"The children have left Christmas stockings
for the animals in the garden.
They've left a little stocking on the door
of every house in Puddle Lane, too."
"So they have!" said the Magician.
"On every door – except their own.
We'll soon see about that.
I've got some presents for them at home.
Come along, Griffle, and give me a hand.
We'll give them a surprise."

Hari and Gita, Sarah and Davy were back,
and were sitting by the fire, when they heard
a loud bang in Puddle Lane.
They rushed to the window, and looked out.

Little stars of light were floating in the air.
The gates at the end of the lane opened,
and someone came through, pulling a sledge.
"It's the Magician!" cried Davy.
"The Magician's back!"
The children ran out into the lane.
"It's Christmas Eve!" cried the Magician.
"Merry Christmas, everyone!"

Music began to play, though no one could see where it came from.
And all the people in Puddle Lane came out of their houses to dance in the snow. There were presents for everyone.

The cats who lived in the Magician's garden
heard the music, and looked out of their hole.
They saw their stocking, and smelt the fishpaste.

The mice who lived in
the hollow tree woke up,
and smelt the cheese.
They rushed up inside
the tree — and there
was their stocking,
full of food, and a
beautiful little cake.

Davy saw a head looking over the wall.

"It's the Griffle!" he cried.

"Merry Christmas, Griffle."

"M-Merry Christmas," said the Griffle.

"And th-thank you for my present.

I – I'll see you tomorrow. I'll go now."

He vanished.

"He was always scared of noise," said Davy.

"What a lovely Christmas Eve," said Gita.
"It's the best we've ever had," said Sarah.
"And we've still got tomorrow," said Davy.
"Tomorrow is Christmas Day!"